THE HOUSESITTER

AN EROTIC ADVENTURE

VICTORIA RUSH

VOLUME 25

JADE'S EROTIC ADVENTURES - BOOK 25

COPYRIGHT

The Housesitter © 2020 Victoria Rush

Cover Design © 2020 PhotoMaras

FEEL THE RUSH:

Jade's Erotic Adventures – Book 1

When lonely divorcée Jade seeks to broaden her horizons, she's invited to a private dinner event which promises to stimulate all of her senses. Wearing nothing but masquerade masks, dinner guests receive special service under the table while their fellow diners look on...

The Dinner Party

Jade's Erotic Adventures - Book 2

Jade discovers an exotic adventure club where strangers meet to explore each other's bodies in mysterious dark rooms. Using special effects to project swirling light patterns onto their figures, the shifting shadows provide just enough illumination to highlight their naked bodies while protecting their identities...

The Dark Room

Jade's Erotic Adventures - Book 3

Jade discovers a yoga club where members stretch and explore each other's bodies in the buff. She books an appointment, and during the first session meets a young redhead who tantalizes her with her flexibility and stunning body...

Naked Yoga

For the uninhibited...

1

As I finished packing my bags for my two-week vacation to Bora Bora, my heart pounded with excitement. I hadn't been away from home for this long in years, and I could already feel the warm sea breeze on my face. Even though it was early March in Chicago, I'd chosen to wear light Bermuda shorts and open sandals so I could enjoy the tropical lifestyle the moment I stepped off the plane. I was ready to leave the melting snow and biting wind-chill of the midwestern winter far behind.

But I was anxious for another reason. I was about to leave the security of my valuable home and the care of my beloved tabby cat in the hands of a teenager I barely knew. I'd seen her grow up over the years as the daughter of my best friend, but this was the first time she'd be responsible for managing an entire household on her own. Granted, her mother lived only a half-hour away, but there was still a lot of mischief a high school senior could get into left to her own devices for so long. I had visions of her holding wild house parties and her friends trashing the place while the neighbors looked on disapprovingly as the cops raided the place.

The only comfort I had was knowing I'd be able to monitor the property 24/7 using my recently installed security system. With five Wi-Fi-enabled cameras installed at key locations in and around the house, I'd be able to watch and listen for any unusual activity directly from my iPhone. I was a bit concerned about invading my housesitter's privacy, but I'd already informed her of the setup and both she and her mother seemed okay with the arrangement.

Besides, it wasn't as if I'd be spying on her in private areas like the bathroom and bedroom. I just wanted to make sure that the main points of ingress and egress were protected and that high-value areas of my house could be watched. I'd had the system installed for *her* safety as much as my own.

Or so I'd convinced myself.

As I carried my suitcases downstairs, I heard the soft chime of the doorbell. I looked at my watch and saw that I had four hours before my flight departure.

Good girl, I thought. She's already demonstrating responsibility by arriving on time for our scheduled briefing. Even though I'd emailed her intricate instructions, there were still a few important details I wanted to go over.

But when I opened the door, I wasn't quite ready for what I saw. The cute freckle-faced teenager I'd known in her youth had blossomed into a beautiful, curvy, full-figured woman. Wearing tight stretch jeans and a form-fitting sweater, she reminded me of the statuesque actress Christina Hendricks from the TV series Mad Men. I hadn't seen her for quite a few months, and she seemed to have a whole new confidence about her.

"Hi Jenny," I stammered, catching my breath. "Please, come in. Do you need some help with your bags?"

"No thanks, Mrs. Jackson," she smiled, lifting her small suitcase, stepping into my vestibule. She had flushed cheeks from the cold weather outside and she rubbed her hands together to warm them up as I closed the door.

"You must be freezing in those light clothes," I said. "Didn't you bring a jacket?"

"I wasn't planning on leaving the house very much," she said. "I've got lots of homework to keep me busy during the school break."

I nodded my head, knowing she was gearing up for college in the fall.

"Yes, I suppose so," I said. "But at least the garage is heated, and you'll have the full use of my car while I'm away if you need anything. So hopefully you'll have minimal exposure to the elements."

"Thanks," Jenny said. "I'll take good care of your property, I promise."

"It'll be good training for college," I smiled. "Is this the first time you've been on your own for this long?"

"Other than the occasional babysitting gig, yes."

"I've stocked up the fridge and left instructions for everything in the kitchen, so hopefully it won't be too much trouble. Why don't you bring your bags and leave them at the bottom of the stairs while I get you up to speed?"

Jenny followed me down the hall and dropped her bags at the landing to my stairs, then I led her into the kitchen and swung open the pantry door.

"The most important thing is making sure Oscar is properly fed and keeping his litter box clean. I've pulled out two cans of cat food and a bag of kibble and placed them on the kitchen island. All the other instructions are on the fridge door."

Oscar jumped up on top of the island when he heard the familiar rustling of his kibble bag, and Jenny rubbed his shoulders while I continued the briefing.

"I give him two scoops of kibble in his dish by the door in the morning and try to keep his water dish at least half-filled with fresh water at all times. Then another half-can of wet food around six p.m. and a few mouthfuls of kibble whenever he seems needy."

"He seems pretty amenable," Jenny said, listening to him purr as she gently stroked his back.

"He's pretty low maintenance," I nodded, happy to see Oscar warming up to her so fast. "Give him a little bit of cuddling a few times a day and he's pretty happy. Let me show you where I keep his litter box."

I led Jenny to my main-floor laundry room and opened a closet door revealing a large bag of cat litter.

"His litter box is under the laundry sink. If you clean it once every couple of days, it will keep the smell under control. Just scoop up any clumps you see with the little ladle and place it in this covered waste can. If it gets full, the trash collection comes every Tuesday and Friday, but honestly it should be fine for the two weeks you're here. If the litter gets low, refill as necessary using this bag."

I pointed to a cat toy resting atop one of the shelves.

"If you feel like playing with him every now and then to keep him from getting bored, he loves playing this little cat-and-mouse game."

I picked up the toy fishing rod and dangled a stuffed mouse above his head while he playfully batted at it. After I placed the device on the dryer, Jenny picked it up and pulled the mouse along the floor in front of Oscar's face as he chased after it. I couldn't help noticing her round ass in her tight jeans as she wiggled her hips to simulate the mouse scurrying along the floor.

"Perfect," I smiled with a slight flush in my face. "You two will be best friends in no time. Of course, you're welcome to use the washer and dryer at your leisure. The controls are pretty self-explanatory."

"I'm used to doing my own laundry, so no problem," Jenny nodded.

I led her back to the kitchen and placed my keys on the island countertop.

"These are the keys to the house and the car. Instructions for the TV remote are on the table beside my sofa. You're also welcome to use my computer in the office if you need to print anything or do some extra homework. The login password is Oscar123."

I glanced into my backyard and motioned to the pool.

"One other thing. I've uncovered the pool a bit early and turned on the water heater, so if you feel like a refreshing swim or want to use the hot tub, feel free any time."

Jenny looked outside and widened her eyes looking at the rippling turquoise water.

"Wow," she said. "I wasn't expecting that. I'm afraid I didn't bring any swim clothes..."

"I've got some swimsuits in my bedroom dresser upstairs. You're welcome to use those." I glanced at Jenny's large breasts and chuckled. "Though I'm not sure you'll fit into them very comfortably."

"I'll find a way to make do," she smiled.

"Okay then," I said, suddenly aware of the twitch in my pussy. "Everything else is pretty self-explanatory, but if you have any questions or run into any trouble you can text me on my phone. I should have it with me most of the time, but if there's an emergency you can also call my neighbor Betty, whose number is on the fridge."

"I hope you won't be looking at your phone *too* much while you're on vacation," Jenny smiled. "Isn't that the whole point of going on vacation? To get away from all those everyday troubles?"

"Of course," I said, pulling my cell phone out of my purse. "I don't intend to, but I wanted to remind you that I've got cameras set up in various places throughout the house to keep an eye on things. I'll be checking in periodically to make sure you're not having any wild parties or burning the place down."

"Not to worry, Mrs. Jackson," Jenny chuckled. "Between the pool, the TV, and the computer, I've got plenty of other things to keep me amused."

I smiled at her, admiring her voluptuous figure.

"There are no cameras in the private areas like as the bedroom and washrooms, so you don't have to worry about your personal privacy." I pointed outside the kitchen door, where a small wireless camera hung from the eavestrough. "But just so you know, one camera keeps an eye on the back-yard, and there's also one at each of the exit doors, and one at the top and bottom of the central stairway, all of which can pan and tilt to provide wide coverage of each area. So you might want to keep your clothes on while you're scam-pering around the house."

"No problem with the cameras," Jenny smiled. "I'm used to having my parents keeping close tabs on me already."

"I'll bet," I said, trying not to undress her with my eyes. "You must be dying to head off to college in a few months.

All those cute boys and toga parties–you'll think you'd died and gone to heaven."

"I'm not really into all that..." Jenny said, shrugging her shoulders.

"Not even *boys*? There'll be a whole new set of rules once you get onto campus."

"We'll see," Jenny said, glancing at my cleavage in my tight cotton blouse. "I'm sure there'll be plenty of other distractions when I get there."

"Um, yes," I said, momentarily taken aback by her sudden change in demeanor. I heard a honk from the driveway and glanced at my watch. "That must be my taxi. Did you have any more questions before I head off for the airport?"

"I think I'm good to go," Jenny said. "Enjoy your trip and don't worry about Oscar or your house. Everything will be just like you left it when you come back."

"Thanks, Jenny," I said, leaning in to give her a peck on the cheek. "Thanks again for looking after things while I'm away. I've transferred four hundred dollars to your account for the initial deposit. I'll pay the second installment when I return."

"Sounds great," Jenny said, cradling a purring Oscar in her arms. "But if everything turns out to be *this* easy, I might have to issue a refund."

"You're going to need every penny you can earn for college," I said. "It's the least I can do."

I carried my bags out to the driveway and the taxi driver placed them in the trunk, then I nestled into the back seat. It wasn't until I sat down that I realized how wet my panties had become. I wasn't sure if it was the feel of Jenny's skin on my lips that had gotten my juices flowing, or her comment about having other distractions at college. Had her glance at my cleavage projected an interest in something other than *boys*?

Either way, something told me that I'd be checking my phone more often than either of us expected while I was on my little South Pacific excursion.

2

———

B y the time I checked in for my flight and cleared through security at the airport, it was already starting to get dark. When I got to the waiting area at my departure gate, I picked up a magazine and tried to distract myself while waiting for the flight to board. But I couldn't stop thinking about Jenny. I was absolutely floored by her transformation from a skinny freckle-faced freshman to a stunning, statuesque high school senior. Not only did she have a figure that made my mouth water, but some of her reactions suggested she was just as interested in me as I was with her.

Did her comment about not being into boys and her frequent glances at my cleavage signal she was attracted to women, like me? And when I mentioned that she might not fit into my bathing suit and she responded by saying that she'd find a way to 'make do', did that mean she was intending to swim in her underwear or–God forbid–in the *buff*?

The more I thought about it, the wetter my panties became as I squirmed uncomfortably in my chair. I glanced up at the display board behind the gate agent's desk and saw that I still had fifteen minutes before the plane began boarding.

What the fuck, I murmured, pulling my phone out of my purse, tapping on the home security app. It won't hurt to check up on her before I depart for the first leg of my flight to Hawaii. If only to make sure Oscar's water bowl is filled.

Yeah, *right*, I smiled, knowing full well that I just wanted to catch another glimpse of her sexy body.

When the app opened, it showed two side-by-side panes displaying the camera locations inside the house. Seeing no sign of Jenny in either picture, I tapped on each one and toggled my finger across the screen to angle the camera to pan the upstairs and downstairs living areas.

Okay, I said, tilting my head. *Maybe she's in the bedroom or the bathroom getting ready to turn in.*

I waited a few minutes, but still seeing no sign of activity, I swiped my thumb to the left to view the two cameras covering the outside doors. She wouldn't have any reason to be outside in the cold weather, unless she'd stepped outside to have a smoke. But she didn't strike me as the type. Shaking my head in dismay, I swiped to the last two images displaying views of the backyard and the garage.

Still no sign of Jenny.

What the hell, I cursed. Where is she hiding? She couldn't have taken off so soon after I'd left. The car was still parked in the garage, so I knew she hadn't gone out for more provisions.

I was just about to tap the playback feature on the inside cameras to track her previous movement when I noticed a shadowy figure moving around the pool image. A curvy girl wearing a terry-cloth robe walked toward the shallow end of the basin, then dropped her robe on the patio and stepped into the steaming water.

"*Holy shit!*" I exclaimed, recognizing her hourglass figure and her long, corkscrew hair. *She's naked! And she's going to skinny dip in my pool!*

The outdoor security camera had detected her movement and turned on the security lamp, illuminating her body like a pale apparition against the reflecting surface of the pool. Covering her breasts with crossed arms over her chest, she slowly lowered herself into the water then began doing gentle breast strokes across the thirty-foot-long pit.

As I watched her silvery body gliding through the water like a translucent nymph, I suddenly became aware of the moisture building up between my legs. Even though I could only see the back of her body partially obscured by the swirling water, I could clearly make out the cleft in her ass and the exquisite curvature of her hips as she flapped her legs in and out in a gentle whipping motion.

Jesus Christ, I panted, imagining she was scissoring her legs against something *else* right now.

When she reached the end of the pool and turned around to swim the opposite length, I could see her pretty face illuminated by the bright spotlight as her head bobbed up and down in the shimmering water.

Oh my God, I muttered under my breath, scarcely believing what I was seeing.

I began to spread my legs unconsciously, imagining her burying her face in my pussy as I watched her beautiful ass rising and falling in the tumbling surf. I placed two fingers on the screen and pinched them together, zooming in on her figure slicing through the water. As she swam back and forth across the pool, I traced her motion by drawing my finger slowly across the screen to turn the camera in lock-step with her movement.

I was so mesmerized by the intoxicating scene on my phone, I barely heard the announcement over the public address system for the last call to board my plane. I looked up, and noticing the diminishing line of passengers streaming onto the jet bridge, I picked up my bags and scurried to the end of the queue.

Fuck! I cursed under my breath, trying to balance my iPhone in my hand while I fumbled with my boarding pass.

I just prayed that I'd be able to access the airport's Wi-Fi signal from inside the plane so I wouldn't have to miss another second of watching her sexy figure.

When I nestled into my seat by the window, I turned my body away from my seatmates and pulled my phone close to my breast so I could watch her without any further interruption. The last thing I needed was for someone to catch me leering at her like I was watching some kind of porn video. But just as Jenny paused by the pool-side ladder preparing to lift herself out of the water, the flight attendant announced over the p.a. system that we had to turn off our electronic devices in preparation for take-off.

You've got to be kidding me, I cursed as I watched Jenny reach up onto the handles.

"Madam?" a flight attendant said, leaning over the aisle. "Please turn off your phone and connect your seat belt. We're about to take off."

I peered up at her with my mouth agape, as if supplicating divine intervention. The timing couldn't have been worse. Just as I tapped the power button on the side of my phone, I saw the top of Jenny's dripping breasts rise out of the pool before the screen faded to black. Gritting my teeth in frustration, I checked the information folder in the back pocket of the seat in front of me to learn how to connect to the airplane's inflight Wi-Fi network. I didn't want to miss one more unnecessary second of spying on this sexy vixen if I could avoid it. Even if she'd gotten dressed by the time I got back online, I could still use the replay button to watch the entire scene from start to finish over and over.

Thank God for modern technology, I said to myself, noticing a large wet spot had formed in the front of my shorts.

F orty-five agonizing minutes later, after the plane had reached cruising altitude, I heard a chime and looked up to see that the seat belt sign had been turned off. It was now okay to power back up my electronic devices. I pressed the power button on my phone, tapping my foot impatiently while I waited for the home screen to light up.

When I saw the familiar apps appear on the screen, I tapped the settings icon then clicked the Wi-Fi function to join the air carrier's proprietary inflight service. They were charging an outrageous $24.99 for a full-flight pass, but at this point I would have paid ten times that amount to get back online. After entering my credit card information and agreeing to the terms, I saw the three delta-shaped bars alight on the top left-hand side of my phone screen.

Okay, we're back in business, I huffed, clicking the home security app until it opened up to the pool-cam view. But when the image appeared, there was no longer any sign of Jenny anywhere in the backyard.

Of course she would have gone back indoors after coming out of the pool, I said to myself. *It's freezing cold at this time of the day in Chicago!*

I was about to tap the replay button so I could watch her naked body slicing through the water again when my finger paused over the glass.

Unless...

Could she have jumped in the hot tub to relax and stay warm after her late evening swim? Could I be that lucky?

I swiped my thumb down to tilt the camera closer to the front of the house, and my heart skipped a beat when I saw Jenny submerged in the churning water with her arms outstretched over the rim. Her body was turned away from the neighbors' yards, directly facing the camera. The top of her tits poked out of the swirling water like two pink balloons, dancing atop the churning eddy.

She had a quiet, blissful look on her face, but I could see her body shifting under the opaque surface of the water. For a moment, I thought it was just the action of the powerful jets pushing against her body from all directions. But there was something about the way she was moving her shoulders and adjusting her position on the seat that led me to believe there was something more going on.

Could she possibly be...?

I knew from plenty of personal experience just how pleasurable it was to position the jets directly in front of my pussy. With the powerful rush of water flowing over my clit, there was nothing quite so heavenly as the feel of the warm water caressing my most sensitive part. When Jenny lowered her hands under the water and angled her arms toward her crotch, there was no longer any doubt.

She was playing with herself under the water!

As I watched her lean her head back against the top of the hot tub and her mouth begin to part open, I suddenly felt a rush of heat and wetness to my own aching pussy.

She certainly didn't waste any time making herself comfortable in my house, I smiled.

But I could tell from her position in the tub that she was missing the ideal placement to receive the most direct stimulation.

Move two feet to your left! I wanted to shout at her while I stared at my phone screen. *There's a jet perfectly positioned to stimulate your clit! You haven't lived until you've come from one of those things!*

I remembered that I'd added a two-way audio feature to each of the cams so I could send a warning message to any potential burglars caught by my motion sensors. For a brief moment, I considered turning it on to encourage her to take full advantage of the hot tub's special features. But this was no *burglar*–this was my young housesitter who must have thought I was far out of earshot by now flying over the Pacific Ocean.

Besides, even if I could reach out to her this way, how could I possibly hope to carry on such an intimate conversation without attracting the suspicion of my fellow passengers sitting only inches away?

But it didn't take long for Jenny to figure it out. Her arms stretched out to her sides as she searching for the precise location of each of the water nozzles. When she leaned forward a few inches and felt the jet shooting up from the edge of the bench a few seats over, she froze for a moment as her eyes widened in excitement. It only took a few seconds for her to move directly over the pulsating stream as she slumped her body lower into the water.

Suddenly, her mouth gaped open as she felt the powerful jet pulsing against her sensitive nub. I knew immediately what she was feeling, and I ached to be lying next to her, feeling her body shaking as she reveled in the rising pleasure administered by the powerful spray. She tilted her head further back against the rim, then her elbows flared out from her sides as she squeezed her tits under the swirling water.

Fuck me, I cursed, wishing it were *my* hands caressing her gorgeous melons instead of her own. I dreamed how I'd ravage her in the sensuous whirlpool while hidden from the prying eyes of my neighbors under the cloak of the swirling water.

I sat captivated as Jenny's mouth gaped progressively wider from the intense pleasure building inside her. When her climax finally washed over her, her head began jerking back and forth while her face scrunched up into the most exquisite form of ecstasy. I almost came along with her, squeezing my thighs tightly together trying to keep my body from writhing in sympathy with her next to my oblivious seat mates.

After she stopped trembling in the swirling water, Jenny lay back against the seat of the hot tub and slumped her shoulders in delirious exhaustion. She had the cutest flush on her face, and for a brief moment, I thought she glanced up at the security camera perched only a few feet away from the tub.

Had she suspected that I was watching her the whole time? Did she notice the movement of the camera as I traced her movement in the pool and the hot tub? Or heard the soft whirring of the camera as I zoomed in on her face when she came?

If so, what was already the most stimulating thing I'd witnessed in a long time, suddenly became even more arousing. I needed to release my pent-up sexual tension, and fast. I peered over at the lavatory sign nearest me and noticed that it was vacant. I waited a few minutes until Jenny stepped out of the hot tub, revealing her glorious glistening body, before I asked to be excused.

The moment I locked the lavatory door behind me, I tore off my clothes and thrust three fingers deep inside my sopping pussy, fucking myself furiously. It must have taken less than ten seconds for me to pop off with the most powerful orgasm I'd had in months. As I stood quivering over the sink with my hand embedded in my snatch, I looked up at the mirror and smiled.

I suddenly knew that I wouldn't be so alone on this trip after all.

3

When I returned to my seat, I switched over to the indoor cams and noticed that Jenny had gone upstairs, flitting back and forth between the master bedroom and bath. She'd changed into flannel pajamas with a Little Mermaid pattern, and I smiled at the contrast of the girly cartoon images with her sexy, curvy figure. The upstairs camera was installed at the top of the stairs, but she'd left the bedroom door ajar just enough for me to angle the camera to see the edge of the bed.

When she emerged from the bathroom, she picked up a book from the nightstand and propped up the pillows to provide a comfortable reading position. Then she sat down on the bed and began reading with her legs crossed over one another. As she wiggled her bare toes while she read, I zoomed in the camera to examine her face more closely.

Her auburn hair fell softly against her pale cheeks in gentle ringlets, highlighting her speckled cheekbones. She had large eyes with brilliant green irises, framed by dark eyebrows arching seductively over long lashes. And her slender nose had a slight upturn at the end, accentuating her puffy rosebud lips and cleft chin. Wearing virtually no makeup, she looked like a fashion doll from a Bergdorf Goodman department store.

The perfect model of young, sensual beauty, I thought.

While she read her book, her gaze stayed focused just below the line of sight of the camera down the hall. As much as I wanted to zoom out to take in more of her breathtaking body, I was afraid the noise might attract her attention and she'd catch me spying on her again. But after a while, she placed the book beside her on the bed and peered around my bedroom, looking for another distraction.

Much to my horror, she leaned over and pulled open the drawer to my bedside night stand. The noise of the drawer gave me an opportunity to zoom back out, and I saw her eyes widen as she peered inside at the contents. I'd thought about hiding my sex toys in another location, but I hadn't imagined she'd be bold enough to go fishing around in my personal effects.

Cheeky girl, I smiled, noticing my breathing rate becoming more raspy.

I kept a whole treasure trove of toys next to the bed, and it must have looked like a veritable candy store to a young teenager just turning the corner into adulthood. She pulled out each device one at a time, examining it closely before placing it on the side of the bed beside her.

The first one was the long and sturdy Magic Wand, my trusty industrial-strength vibrator that delivered a powerful and sustained jolt directly to the clitoris. She held the handle vertically in her left hand and gripped the flexible ball at the top, bending it forward and back with her other hand. Then she pulled out my tiny Pocket Rocket and twisted the end, feeling the nubby head beginning to buzz softly in her hand. When she reached in and removed the salami-sized, two-sided silicone dildo that I used whenever I had a special friend over, I grimaced in embarrassment. She grasped the double-headed penis at each end and bent it forward and back into a U-shape, pinching her eyebrows and shaking her head in dismay.

It must have been a shock to her young sensibilities to discover all the naughty ways a woman could stimulate herself with the wide assortment of sex aids on the market. Or maybe she was just trying to fathom how the demure Mrs. Jackson, who she'd known since childhood, had become such a perverted sex addict.

Not so demure now, am I little girl? I smiled, feeling my juices beginning to flow again in my tight Bermuda shorts.

She reached back into the drawer and pulled out a strange-looking device that looked like a balled fist with two fingers pointing up in a V-shape. Jenny held up my familiar JimmyJane vibrator and inserted her finger between the two appendages. Then she tapped the button on the base and smiled as the little digits fluttered against her hand.

Mmm, yes, I nodded toward the screen. *It feels even better when you place your clit between the vibrating fingers.*

I was getting increasingly worked up watching my young housesitter play with each of the devices, wondering when she was going to try them in the manner they were intended.

She placed the JimmyJane vibrator down on the mattress, then removed a U-shaped object from the drawer and looked at it with a wrinkled brow. She grasped the two ends of the We-Vibe toy and gently flexed it open a few inches. Then she began tapping the buttons on the outside of the device to feel the different vibration settings on each side.

Did she even know which end to put inside? I wondered. She didn't look like she'd had much experience using vibrators. For all I knew, she'd only seen those hard plastic phallic-shaped dildos still prominently displayed in most sex shop windows.

At least she's got a full two weeks to experiment with them, I smiled.

Knowing the best was yet to come, I saw her lean over and extract one of my favorite sex toys, the Rabbit. Shaped like an oversize erect penis, it had a transparent shaft with circulating beads and a protruding thumb-shaped arm with two soft silicone rabbit ears that fluttered against the clitoris. Jenny picked it up and tapped each of the control buttons on the base, watching with amazement as the head of the dildo wobbled like a spinning top while the chrome beads rotated in the middle of the shaft and the rabbit ears fluttered softly against her palm.

Yeah, girl, I smiled. *That one will put you over the top in no time.*

I was intrigued why Jenny hadn't started to experiment with any of the toys by removing her clothes, but I was thrilled that she was showing so much interest in my special collection.

She turned her head toward the open drawer and pinched her eyebrows, peering at the last item in the drawer. When she pulled it out, I smiled, recognizing the distinctive shape of the Ose vibrator. Shaped like a giant flexed finger with a flat base harboring a mysterious hole, she must have wondered how in God's name it worked. But as she began tapping the buttons on the base of the unit, her eyes widened as she watched the long finger begin to flex in a come-hither motion.

But it wasn't until she pressed the button controlling the

lower part that her eyes really opened in shock and amazement. As it began to pulse in her hand, she drew it closer and squinted at the little hole, watching it pucker in and out like some kind of animatronic mouth. Which is exactly what it was designed to simulate. This was one of my favorite vibrators for exactly that reason, and for a moment I was disappointed that I hadn't packed it for my trip.

But when I saw Jenny pull down her pajama bottoms and spread her knees apart, I quickly forgot about my own needs as I zoomed in to inspect her sex. I gasped when I saw that she'd shaved herself entirely bare, and my pussy spasmed when I saw her glistening pink folds framing her pretty flower.

When she picked up the Ose vibrator and pointed the finger toward her hole, I shifted uncomfortably in my narrow airplane seat, dying to rip off my clothes and spread my legs far apart while I fucked myself watching her. When she inserted the wand into her slit, I groaned audibly, and the woman sitting next to me turned her head, momentarily distracted from the book she was reading.

But when Jenny thrust the device deep into her pussy and tapped the buttons to activate the two human-like functions, I sat up and cleared my throat, trying to keep myself composed. But the rivers of lubrication running down the inside of my thighs made it clear I was anything but composed. I pulled a magazine out of the seat flap in front of me and placed it on my lap to conceal the rapidly darkening wet spot in the crotch of my shorts, turning the phone screen even further away from the prying eyes of the passengers around me. Even though I'd be absolutely mortified if anyone caught me watching the video, there was no way in hell I could stop now, even if the air marshal tried to force me to put it away. They'd have to send in a virtual *army* to wrench this live feed out of my hands.

With the Ose vibrator now pulsing at full speed against Jenny's pussy, she pulled her knees up closer toward her chest and spread her legs further apart. The sight of the fluttering object planted between her legs as she threw her head back against the pillows was driving me insane with desire. But when she unbuttoned the top of her pajamas and began twisting the teats on her voluptuous tits, I couldn't take it anymore.

I excused myself once again, saying I had an upset stomach, and headed back to the lavatory with my phone in hand. As I waited impatiently for the occupant to come out, I inserted my earbuds into the port on the bottom of my phone and tapped the screen to engage the audio function. I could hear Jenny moaning into my ear, and I flapped my legs impatiently, desperately wanting to get into the private room where I could relieve myself.

When the passenger finally opened the door and began to step out, I practically ran him over squeezing into the chamber, slamming the door shut. I placed the phone on top of the sink and pulled my shorts down to my ankles and thrust two fingers into my snatch, pulling the base of my hand hard up against my throbbing clit. As I watched Jenny's knees beginning to flutter with increasing urgency and a deep flush begin to spread over the top of her bosom, I couldn't hold it any longer. As my orgasm washed over me like a tidal wave, I gushed all over my hand and fingers, shaking like I was having an epileptic seizure.

Soon after, Jenny's body also began to convulse as she groaned in the throes of her own powerful climax. As I watched her firm melons bouncing on her chest and her face flush a deep shade of crimson, I moaned along with her until we were both completely spent and exhausted. Then I peered down at my dripping thighs and drenched shorts lying on the floor, wondering how I'd ever be able to return to my seat in such a messy condition. There was no way I could wear these same shorts drenched in my lubrication and God knows how many other people's dried urine from the lavatory floor. There was only one way out of here.

Opening the door a crack, I waited until a female flight attendant passed by, then I quietly called out to her. She turned toward me with a puzzled look and came closer to my door.

"I'm so sorry to bother you about this," I said. "But I've had a bit of an accident and I'm afraid I won't be able to wear these shorts again for the rest of the flight."

She widened her eyes and nodded knowingly. Apparently, I wasn't the only passenger who'd run into this predicament before.

"Can I ask you a huge favor?" I said. "Could you retrieve my carry-on bag from the overhead storage compartment above seat 15F? It's tan colored and has a name tag for J. Jackson."

"No worries, Mrs. Jackson," she said. "I'll be back with your bag in just a moment."

When she returned with my case, I placed it on top of the small vanity and wiped down my legs with a moist towelette. Then I stepped out of my soiled shorts and threw them in the waste receptacle.

I won't be needing those anymore, I murmured to myself. The hard part would be keeping my dick in my pants for the *rest* of the flight to Hawaii. I knew that I'd have to find another distraction to keep me busy so I didn't soil another pair of shorts.

No more Jenny videos until I get to my own private room, I said.

But my mind was already swimming with all the new entertainment possibilities over the course of the next two weeks.

Who needs tropical beaches and chilled mai tai's when you've got the most beautiful, sexy lingerie model at your beck and call whenever you need her?

4

—————

After changing into fresh clothes, I returned to my seat by the window. Even though I was dying to see what Jenny would do next, I dared not reopen the camera app for fear of making another mess. For the rest of the flight to Hawaii, I kept myself distracted watching a movie. A very tame, family-oriented movie. I didn't want to risk viewing another sexy scene that might rekindle my new obsession with my young housesitter.

When we landed in Hawaii, I had to change planes for the next leg of my flight to Bora Bora, so there wasn't any time to check the home security monitors during the brief stopover. By the time I boarded the aircraft, I was so exhausted, I slept the rest of the way to my final destination. When I landed in the archipelago, I took a taxi to my hotel, where a porter escorted me to an overwater bungalow overlooking a turquoise lagoon. I hadn't eaten for eight hours, so I unpacked my bags then headed to the dining room for a sumptuous seafood dinner.

By the time I returned to my room half-intoxicated on margaritas, I was ready to power up my phone and resume watching my new favorite playmate. But with the five-hour time difference between Bora Bora and Chicago, Jenny was already fast asleep, nestled under the warm covers of my bed. It hardly mattered though, since by now I had almost a full day's worth of video to play back any time I wanted.

I tapped the home monitoring app on my phone and toggled back to the upstairs view. I'd left the camera pointed in the direction of the bedroom, so I hoped there'd be plenty more footage of Jenny amusing herself with my toys. But I was disappointed to see that after coming so hard using the Ose vibrator, she'd put the rest of the instruments away before turning in.

I guess after having two powerful back-to-back orgasms, she needed a rest, I smiled. *Or maybe she was just pacing herself, leaving room to enjoy the other devices another day.*

I came three more times replaying the erotic scenes from the hot tub and my bedroom, over and over. When I finally satiated my lust, I took a relaxing dip in my room's private plunge pool, watching the sun set over the quiet lagoon.

I could get used to this, I thought, taking in the blissful scene.

The only thing missing was a partner to enjoy it with. Maybe I'd bring Jenny back with me next time. The only problem was her mother, who just happened to be my best friend. I didn't want to risk damaging our longstanding relationship. Even if Jenny *had* recently turned eighteen and could make her own decisions.

I fell asleep that night feeling the warm ocean breeze wafting through my veranda window, dreaming of Jenny's naked body gliding through the coral waters of my lagoon. When I woke up, it was already past noon Chicago time, and I flipped over my phone to see what she was up to. I found her sitting at the kitchen island with some school books propped open, making notes in her journal.

Good girl. You don't want to waste your entire spring break playing around the house. You'll need good marks to get into your choice of college in the fall. There'll be plenty of other distractions to keep you amused when you get there.

I walked down to the breakfast bar in the hotel and helped myself to a large serving of eggs Benedict with a side of fresh pineapple and lox. I almost felt sorry leaving Jenny with a fridge full of microwave dinners and pre-cooked casseroles. But something told me she'd find *other* ways to keep herself satisfied while I was away.

I needed to find something to keep my mind off what was happening back home, so I signed up for a snorkeling expedition to a nearby reef. When we arrived there, I marveled at the variety of colorful sea creatures, from striped angelfish to iridescent snapper and giant speckled grouper. I loved swimming among the docile nurse sharks and stingrays, even hitching a brief ride on a large sea turtle. After returning to my room and noticing that I was already a bit sunburned, I pulled off my wet bathing suit and propped myself up in my bed.

When I checked in on Jenny, at first I couldn't see any sign of her in the main rooms of the house or in the back-yard. It took a few minutes of angling the upstairs and downstairs cams before I saw her seated in my office, quietly tapping on my keyboard. Although the door was slightly ajar, the line of sight from the ceiling-mounted camera to the office only allowed me to see half of her body.

I remembered leaving my login code if she needed to print anything, but the audio feed didn't indicate any sign of activity other than soft tapping on the keyboard. I hesitated for a moment, thinking I'd give her some peace and quiet and check back later in the evening. Maybe I'd catch her using another one of my sex toys when it was closer to bedtime.

But then I remembered I had *another* app on my phone that provided direct access to my home computer. It was useful when I needed to access important files remotely, but I hadn't used it for a long time. I clicked on the app, and it opened showing my live screen with Jenny's cursor hovering near the top of the web browser. She clicked on the bookmarks tab and began scrolling through my list of saved web addresses.

Forgetting that I'd arranged everything into themed folders, I was mortified when she clicked on the folder for my favorite lesbian porn videos. I used these whenever I felt particularly horny and needed a distraction, but I never intended for anyone *else* to find my private stash. She double-clicked on a link labeled *hot tribbing*, and a window opened showing two naked girls scissoring on an oversize bed. Jenny tapped on the speaker icon at the bottom of the screen and slid the volume bar to the right, and I heard soft moaning wafting out into the hall.

Unsure if it was Jenny's voice or the sounds of the girls on the video, I toggled back to the camera monitoring app. Jenny's left leg was spread far apart with her jeans pulled down to her ankles as she rolled her hips sensuously on the chair. Unable to see what she was doing from the rear position of the camera and with her back turned away from me, I cursed at my inability to watch her more closely. Desperately wanting to see what she was doing while she watched the video, I scanned the remote access menu and noticed a camera icon.

When I clicked the button, my iPhone screen divided into a split window with the tribbing video on one side and

Jenny's face on the other. I could only see the top half of her body from the fixed position of the webcam atop my laptop, but that was more than enough. Her cheeks were flushed as she squeezed one of her breasts with her right hand and extended her other arm between her legs in a rhythmic motion.

Holy fuck! I groaned. She was playing with herself while watching a lesbian porn video!

There was no longer any doubt in my mind that she was sexually attracted to women. As I watched her face twist into increasing contortions of pleasure, my eyes darted back and forth between the scene playing out on the porn video and the expression on her face. As the girls on the video began rubbing their pussies together more vigorously, I suddenly heard a familiar buzzing sound coming from the background.

Was she fucking herself with one of my vibrators while she watched the video?

I switched back to the security camera view, but all I could see was Jenny's left leg shaking while her free arm pumped something between her legs. Suddenly overcome with desire, I rushed over to my suitcase and pulled out the one vibrator I'd had the foresight to pack for the trip—my trusty Lelo G-spot stimulator. I thrust the gently curved rod into my snatch and turned the vibration setting up high as I flipped back to the screen monitoring app.

I could hear Jenny moaning along with the two girls on the video as her oversize melons began to tremble from the rising pleasure emanating within her. When the girls suddenly locked their hips, pulling each other tightly toward one another screaming in unison, Jenny's mouth gaped apart, and she uttered a deep guttural groan. With her body jerking forward and back in rhythmic contractions, I grabbed my long dildo with two hands and clamped down on it as I came hard along with Jenny.

It must have taken a full minute for both of us to stop spasming and cumming from the erotic scene we'd both witnessed. I smiled at the irony of getting off watching Jenny while she watched the girls on the video. My mind reeled with all the possibilities for engagement between the two of us when I returned home. Suddenly I realized Jenny was no longer just an innocent high school student, but a fully developed woman, ready to experiment with all the different ways of satisfying her sexual curiosity.

Fortunately for me, Jenny was far from finished quenching her desire for the evening. I saw her right hand move back to the cursor, and she tapped on the progress bar to return to the middle of the video. As it began replaying, she slid the slider slowly to the right until it reached the part where the two girls began pulling their bodies together in preparation for their mutual orgasm.

Jenny peered down, and I heard a deeper kind of throbbing sound emanating from between her legs. As the girls in the video began moaning more loudly, she moved both of her hands between her legs, pounding her pussy with hard jerking motions. I couldn't be sure which vibrator she was using, but the sight of her fucking herself while watching the two girls soon had me thrusting my Lelo vibrator back inside my own pussy. As the girls moved closer to their moment of climax, Jenny's face scrunched up into a painful grimace.

She seemed to be waiting for them to cum once again before she opened the taps. When they finally did, her orgasm was even stronger as she wailed in unison with the girls, jerking her arms forcefully against her body and her compressed tits as she quivered in the office chair. I screamed along with her, feeling my juices spraying out the sides of my pulsating pussy all over my wet thighs and ass.

After Jenny recovered from her second powerful orgasm, she closed the porn site and flipped the laptop cover closed. No longer being able to see her directly, I switched over to the hall cam view, watching her pull up her jeans as she raised herself from the chair. Then she turned around and exited the office, walking toward the stairs. In her right hand, I could see the familiar outline of my purple Rabbit vibrator with its distinctive protruding ears.

I smiled as I watched her head back upstairs to return the vibrator to my nightstand.

That's it, baby, I said. *Take your time trying out each of my special toys. Neither of us is going anywhere for the next two weeks.*

5
———

Jenny went to sleep soon after watching the lesbian video, and I decided to go for a relaxing swim in the lagoon to wind down. Between the day's snorkeling activity, a little too much sun, and multiple orgasms watching Jenny on constant replay, I slept like a baby that night. When I woke the following morning, she was back at the kitchen table doing her homework, so I went for another long breakfast at the hotel restaurant.

Since Jenny seemed to be preoccupied with her studies, I decided to make the best use of my time by taking a sailing tour of the island. Wearing a long-sleeved linen shirt, capri pants, and plenty of sunscreen, I wasn't taking any chances at getting more sunburned. With Jenny becoming increasingly bold with her sexual escapades back home, I wanted to make sure I could enjoy watching her without any distractions.

I was surprised how large the island was, taking us more than six hours to circumnavigate the atoll in our sleek, forty-foot catamaran. Formed by an extinct volcano, lush green hillsides rose steeply above the water to over two thousand feet above sea level. I marveled at how clear the water was as I gazed at the endless variety of colorful fish through the sturdy nets joining the two hulls. But by the time we'd finished our mid-day picnic on a secluded beach, I was ready to get out of the sun and back to the relative tranquility of my private cabin.

When the sailboat returned to the hotel, it was already early evening Chicago time, and I was eager to see what mischief Jenny had gotten into while I was away. After I got back to my bungalow, I turned on my phone and saw her taking a swim in the backyard pool wearing a skimpy cream-colored bikini. Looking like a young Ursula Andress from the famous beach scene in the James Bond movie *Dr. No*, she looked even *more* mouth-watering partially covered up.

But this time she wasn't alone. She'd invited a young friend over, and as the two girls splashed each other's faces in the pool, my pussy twitched at the sight of the two scantily clad teens. When they got out of the pool, they moved over to the hot tub, where Jenny encouraged her friend to try out the special seat she'd used the previous day. I could see the look of surprise on her girlfriend's face when she felt the gush of the underwater jet flowing between her legs, but she didn't seem interested in staying there long enough to get properly aroused.

Whether she felt self-conscious stimulating herself in front of her girlfriend or Jenny had warned her that I could be monitoring the property, I wasn't sure. But either way, I enjoyed watching the girls' pretty faces as the swirling water flowed over the tops of their bikini-clad bodies. Just to be safe, I kept the camera zoomed out and the audio turned off for fear of signaling that I was watching them. But they seemed to be enjoying themselves, chatting and giggling as they sipped what looked like two wine coolers.

Thank you, Jenny's girlfriend, I said, *for bringing the alcohol and Jenny's swimsuit.* I hoped it would be just the right combination for loosening the two girls up and taking this spring break adventure to the next level.

After twenty minutes or so of lounging in the tub, the two girls scurried out of the tank and dried themselves off in the kitchen, then headed upstairs to get changed. I followed their movement with the inside cameras, and when they got to my bedroom, I turned on the upstairs audio feed so I could hear what they were saying.

Jenny peeled off her swimsuit then flipped open my nightstand drawer and pointed inside.

"Guess what I discovered last night while I was in Mrs. Jackson's bed?" she said.

Jenny's friend peered into the drawer, then looked up at Jenny with wide eyes.

"Holy shit!" she said. "Are those what I think they are?"

"I can assure you they absolutely are," Jenny smiled.

"But they all look so *different*," her friend said. "I've only seen those gross penis-shaped vibrators. How do these things even *work*?"

Jenny peeled off her swimsuit and jumped on the bed, patting the mattress beside her.

"Why don't you come join me and find out? Some of these devices are really incredible. Don't tell me you've never tried one before."

"Nothing like *that*, that's for sure," her friend said, hesitating.

Jenny reached into the drawer and pulled out the tiny Pocket Rocket vibrator.

"Come on, Niki," she said. "It's just us girls. No one's ever going to know if we have a little extra fun on our sleepover."

"What if Mrs. Jackson's watching on her home security cam?"

Jenny peered down the hallway toward my camera at the top of the stairs, and I quickly turned it so it was facing the other way.

"There's only one camera on each floor, and it can't see in here anyway," Jenny said. "Take your swimsuit off and join me on the bed. We deserve a little break from all our studying."

I heard the sound of clothes dropping to the floor followed by a bed squeaking as her friend joined her on the bed. Then I slowly swiped my finger across the screen, turning the camera back in their direction. Niki was more petite than Jenny, with a typically slender high-school figure. She looked to be about average height and build, but with firm, perky breasts and athletic, toned legs. She sat leaning back against the headboard, with her arms crossed over her chest and her legs extended close together in front of her.

Jenny twisted the base of the Pocket Rocket then handed it to her friend, who ran her fingers over the buzzing end.

"Pretty cool, right?" Jenny said, smiling at Niki, glancing between her legs. "Don't be so bashful. Give it a try."

Niki angled her knees slightly apart and placed the nubby end of the vibrator at the top of her slit, then she suddenly jumped.

"I *know*, right?" Jenny said. "That little thing packs quite a punch, doesn't it?"

"Mmm," Niki nodded, spreading her legs a little further apart.

"You can adjust the intensity of the vibrations by turning

the cap on the base of the unit. "I like to ramp it up the more turned on I get."

"How many of these things have you *tried* so far?" Niki said, squirming her hips on the mattress.

"Almost all of them. This is nothing compared to some of the *dual-purpose* vibrators."

"Dual purpose?" Niki said, pinching her eyebrows.

"Most of the other ones stimulate you on the inside and the outside at the same time. You haven't experienced a proper orgasm until you've tried one of these things."

"Why did you give me this *little* one to start with then?" Niki panted, obviously beginning to feel the effects of the targeted stimulation on her clit.

"I didn't want to scare you away too fast," Jenny smiled. "Are you ready to step it up?"

"Definitely," Niki grunted.

"Reach in and take out that pink one that looks like a curled-up snake. I think you're going to like the way it moves inside you."

Niki peered into the drawer and shook her head.

"There's two pink objects that look kind of similar," she said. "Which one?"

"Both," Jenny smiled. "We *both* might be able to get in on the action with this one."

Niki pulled the two objects out of the drawer then Jenny took the smaller piece out of her hand.

"What exactly am I supposed to do with this thing?" Niki said, examining the U-shaped We-Vibe device.

"You slide the fat end inside you with the thinner end pointing up. Then press it all the way up until the connecting part is resting against your opening."

"What are you going to do with the *other* attachment?" Niki said.

"You'll see," Jenny said, flashing her a devilish smile.

Up to this point, I'd just been following the playful banter of the two friends as they tried out the tamer device. But when Niki spread her legs further apart and inserted the thick end of the We-Vibe into her slit, I tore off my pants and reached over for my Lelo vibrator resting on the nightstand. Then I watched Niki press the device deep into her hole until the narrower end rested near the base of her mound.

"This feels kind of weird," Niki said, shaking her head. "How do I turn it on?"

"Leave that up to *me*," Jenny smirked, grasping the remote-control unit and tapping one of the buttons.

"You mean you can–*oh!*" Niki grunted, feeling the internal arm of the We-Vibe unit pulsing against the inside of her pussy.

"Damn straight, girl," Jenny said. "I *told* you Mrs. Jackson has an interesting collection of toys. Let me take the driver's seat while you sit back and enjoy the scenery."

"Mmm," Niki purred, glancing at Jenny's voluptuous tits. "You know I've always fantasized about being with you this way. You have the most amazing body..."

Jenny suddenly leaned over and placed her mouth over one of Niki's tits, sucking her pink teats.

"Oh God, Jenny," Niki panted. "That feels so good..."

"You have *no* idea," Jenny said, flicking her finger over the control knob, activating the clitoral stimulator.

"*Uhnn,*" Niki grunted, rolling her hips on the bed as Jenny nibbled her tits and neck. "Fuck me Jenny. Make me come with your hot tongue."

"All in due course, baby," Jenny purred. "I just want you to enjoy this little toy a little longer until you warmed up."

"Oh, I'm getting *warmed up*, alright," Niki groaned,

running her fingers through Jenny's hair. "I'm going to cum soon if you keep that up."

"You mean *this*?" Jenny said, flipping the control switch, raising the intensity of the two vibrating arms.

"*Yes!*" Niki panted, thrashing her hips as Jenny suckled on her nubs.

"Oh my God," Niki hissed. "I'm going to come, Jenny. Suck my tits while I cum!"

Suddenly, Niki grabbed the back of Jenny's head with two hands, pulling her face hard against her chest, spreading her legs as far apart as they could go. I zoomed in, watching the vibrator buzzing against her pussy as she slowly lifted her hips off the bed.

"Uhnn!" she groaned, as her orgasm took over her body. "*Oh God, oh God, oh God!*"

Jenny pulled back and peered up at her friend, watching the look of ecstasy wash over her face as she quivered over the bed. When Niki finally dropped her hips back down onto the mattress, Jenny turned the vibrator off and straddled her hips, kissing her passionately.

"*Fuck*, that was hot," she said, nibbling Niki's ear. "I knew you'd enjoy these things."

"Not nearly as much as I like *you*," Niki said, grabbing Jenny's ass and pulling her closer as she pressed her tits against Jenny's breasts. "Can we put away the toys now and just concentrate on touching each other?"

"I thought you'd never ask," Jenny smiled, grinding her pussy against Niki's bare mound.

"I love the feeling of your body up against me," Niki panted. "I want to feel you fucking me *straight up* this time. I'm so wet right now."

"I can tell," Jenny said, sliding her body down Niki's

abdomen, pressing her thighs apart until her chest rested against Niki's vulva.

"Rub your tits against me, Jenny," Niki pleaded, squirming her hips against Jenny's mounds.

Jenny raised herself up a few inches and grasped one of her globes with two hands, rubbing it playfully up and down Niki's slit.

Up to this point I'd just been rubbing my Lelo vibrator gently against my opening as I absent-mindedly watched the two girls interact. But when I saw Jenny tit-fucking her friend with her voluptuous breasts, I plunged the G-spot stimulator deep into my pussy, rolling it around as I moaned along with Niki.

"*Fuck*," she groaned. "That feels *way* better than a plastic vibrator. You're so warm and wet."

"You know what *also* feels warmer and wetter than a vibrator?" Jenny said, pushing Niki's knees up toward her chest, then lowering her hips over her friend's splayed pussy. As she placed her ass over Niki's twitching vulva, their pussies touched, and they groaned loudly.

"Jesus," Niki gasped. "Where did you learn to do this? Have you been holding out on me?"

"I've been studying a bit more than just math and chemistry since I've been here," Jenny purred, rolling her hips over Niki's upturned cunny.

"*Holy fuck!*" Niki groaned, feeling Jenny's clit pressing against her own. "This is the hottest thing I've ever done. I never even imagined–"

Jenny leaned forward, engulfing Niki's mouth with her own, pressing her tits against the other girl while the two of them ground their pussies together. I could hear the sexy slurping noises of their wet vulvas sliding over one another as their pink folds spread open for my camera. As they picked up the pace of their rocking motion, they moaned into each other's mouths and Niki wrapped her arms around Jenny's back, digging her fingernails into her skin.

Moments later, they both began squealing as their hips trembled in unison. I zoomed in as far as the camera would go, and just as Niki let out a high-pitched scream, Jenny began squirting all over her friend's perineum as Niki's rosebud puckered in and out. In all my years of watching lesbian trib videos, I'd never seen anything so sexy and raw. As I lay exhausted, drenched in my own pool of cum, I reached over and patted the sheet beside me.

If only you were here with me, I thought, imagining Jenny's body merging with my *own* instead of her friend's. *This trip to paradise isn't be complete without you.*

6

Niki went home the following day and for the rest of my vacation I watched old clips of Jenny playing with my toys. She'd occasionally take out a new one and pleasure herself on my bed or while watching lesbian videos, but I soon longed to be next to her, touching her directly. As I neared the end of my trip, I feared I'd lose her forever once the break was over, so I rescheduled my return flight and came home a day early.

When I got to the front door, I didn't feel comfortable barging in on her unannounced, so I tapped the doorbell. She came to the door wrapped in a large bath towel, and her eyes widened as she paused in the doorway.

"Mrs. Jackson!" she said. "I wasn't expecting you until tomorrow. Is everything okay?"

"Yes," I said, feeling Oscar rubbing himself against the bottom of my leg. "I was just feeling a bit sorry for you having to look after this big house all by yourself. I figured you could use an extra day getting ready to return to school."

"I've been studying hard," Jenny said, "so you needn't

have worried. But come in out of the cold–it's your house after all."

"I didn't want to just barge in unannounced. I hope I didn't interrupt you in the middle of anything..."

"Actually, I was just getting ready to take another dip in your pool. It's been such a pleasure enjoying the heated water during the cool evenings."

I smiled, peering at Jenny's hourglass figure in the towel.

"And the hot tub too, I hope. It's a singular pleasure soaking in the stimulating bath when it's cold outside."

"Absolutely," Jenny nodded. "Your place is like a virtual playground for a starved teenager like me."

"Tell you what," I said. "Why don't I drop off my stuff in the bedroom and join you there in a few minutes? I could use another dip in the warm water to ease my transition back to the Chicago weather."

"Sure," Jenny said, noticing my erect nipples in my linen blouse from the chill outside. "Should I get changed?"

"It's starting to get dark, so the neighbors shouldn't be able to spy on us. I don't know about you, but I always enjoy soaking in the hot tub in the raw. It's just us girls, after all."

"I agree," Jenny smiled. "I'll meet you there in a few minutes."

I rushed upstairs and tore off my clothes, then threw on a robe and headed downstairs. When I opened the door to the veranda, Jenny had already submerged herself in the tub, and she peered up at me with dripping hair.

"You certainly look like you've made yourself at home," I smiled, dropping my robe and stepping into the swirling water a few feet away from her.

"It's been kind of fun, actually," she said. "I almost don't want to go back home. I could get used to hanging around here a little longer."

My heart skipped a beat, wondering if I should ask her to stay another night.

"Did you have any trouble operating any of the equipment?" I said, making a veiled reference to my sex toy collection. "Has everything been okay with the pool, the car, and other devices?"

"Yes," Jenny smiled. "Good on all fronts. Were you able to check in periodically to make sure I wasn't burning your house down?"

"Once in a while," I said. "I didn't want to interfere with your privacy too much. Mostly just to check that you were safe and well stocked up."

"I've been able to keep everything replenished pretty well," Jenny nodded. "Thanks to the use of your car. Thanks again for letting me have the use it."

"My pleasure," I said. "Have you been able to get out and see many of your friends while I was away?"

"Not too much," Jenny said. "I had a friend come over for a sleepover one night to help break up the monotony."

"Did you show her around and avail yourselves of all the amenities?" I said, resisting the temptation to let her know just how much I knew she'd enjoyed that sleepover.

"Yes," Jenny blinked. "We went for a swim, had a relaxing hot tub–"

"Did you discover the special *nozzle*?" I smiled.

"You mean–"

"The one that sprays in a particularly delightful place."

"It was hard *not* to," Jenny blushed. "Once you find the right spot, you don't exactly want to move."

"And your *friend*? Did she discover it too?"

"Yes, but I think she was a bit self-conscious about trying it in my presence. I think that's something meant to be enjoyed more by yourself..."

"I don't know about *that*," I said, shifting my body over in front of the spigot. "I kind of missed this while I was away. Do you mind–?"

"Not at all," Jenny smiled. "After all, it's just us girls, right?"

"Right," I said, spreading my legs apart and shifting my weight forward to direct the spray onto my buzzing clit. "Mmm, yes–this is one luxury they didn't have at my expensive resort in Bora Bora."

"It must have been fun though," Jenny said, watching the expression on my face as I squirmed under the water. "There must have been lots of other exciting things to do there."

"I guess so," I said, catching my breath. "Snorkeling, sailing, swimming in the lagoon. It gets pretty old though when you're by yourself. I found myself checking in with you just to keep myself company."

"I hope you didn't catch me skinny dipping in your pool."

"I did indeed," I panted. "And in the hot tub. It looked like you were enjoying yourself as much as I am right now."

"I thought *maybe* you were watching me," Jenny said. "I caught the cameras pointed in my direction a few times."

"Did you *like* being watched?" I said.

"Sometimes," Jenny said. "It was kind of *stimulating* to be honest, knowing you were catching me occasionally without any clothes on."

"Oh yes," I groaned. "I caught you more than once."

"Did you enjoy watching me as much as I liked the idea of you watching me?" Jenny said, lifting an eyebrow.

"You have no idea," I panted. "Almost as much as I am right now."

"Mmm," Jenny said, dipping her hands below the surface of the water and shifting her weight on the seat opposite me.

"I wish I could have spied on *you* as much as you were with me. You know, I always kind of had a thing for you, even when I was little. I always thought you were the most beautiful woman I'd ever seen."

"Oh my God, Jenny," I said, getting even more turned on knowing she found me attractive. "You've blossomed into the most beautiful, sexy young adult. *You're* the one I've had a crush on since you came over to my place."

"Oh Mrs. Jackson," Jenny panted, her cheeks beginning to flush.

"I think it's time you started calling me Jade," I smiled. "Seeing as how we're both stimulating ourselves under the water while watching each other."

"Jade," Jenny purred. "You have no idea how often I've fantasized about you."

"I must have come a hundred times thinking about you while I was away," I said. "I've wanted to feel your body against mine practically from the moment I left."

"Yes," Jenny moaned. "You're going to make me cum watching you."

"Yes, baby," I hissed. "Let it go. I'm almost there too."

"Uhnn," Jenny groaned, spreading her mouth wide open as she looked at me with glazed eyes.

Suddenly, I felt a bolt of electricity running through me as my orgasm washed over me. While we jerked and moaned together in simultaneous climax under the swirling water, we couldn't take our eyes off each other.

"Oh my God," Jenny panted after we both calmed down. "That was *so* hot."

"Let's get the hell out of here and go upstairs where we can do this *properly*," I said. "I need to feel a *warm body* next to me, not just an artificial water jet."

"I was thinking exactly the same thing," Jenny smiled.

The two of us scampered out of the hot tub and ran upstairs, giggling like two girls. When we got to the bed, I didn't even bother to pull down the covers, pulling her onto the mattress with me and entangling our legs together. It was electrifying feeling her naked body rubbing against mine, and for the longest time I was content to rub our slippery bodies together while we kissed passionately. The feeling of Jenny's big tits pressing against mine was sublime, and I was in no hurry to get down to more serious business.

But after a while, I felt Jenny's hands roaming lower on my body, and when her hand slipped into the cleft under my ass, I pulled back and looked at her.

"Jenny," I panted. "You have no idea how much I've wanted to feel your touch on my body.

"And yours on mine," Jenny grinned.

When she slipped two fingers into my hole, I squeezed her tits with two hands, pinching her large teats with my fingers.

"Uhnn," I groaned, feeling my juices spreading all over her hand. "I want to fuck you so bad."

"Yes please," Jenny said.

I pulled her hand out of my pussy, then pushed her down onto the bed and straddled her crotch with my thighs on either side of her hips.

"Does this position look familiar?" I said.

Jenny's eyes widened as she peered up at me with a look of shock.

"*No way!* You weren't watching me and my girlfriend when we were in your bedroom?!"

"I hope you don't mind," I nodded. "You did leave the door open just enough for my camera to zoom in from down the hallway."

"I was kind of hoping you were," Jenny smiled. "Did you see us playing with your toys too?"

"Absolutely," I grinned. "Your girlfriend is almost as hot as you are."

"Maybe the three of us can try this sometime," Jenny said. "I think she's become attracted to girls as much as I have since I've been here."

"Maybe another time," I said. "Right now, I just want to look at your magnificent body while I fuck you with my pussy."

"Yes, Jade," Jenny purred. "Fuck me with your pussy. I want to feel you cumming against me this time."

I rolled Jenny onto her side, pulling her right leg up onto my chest, then I tilted my hips forward until our pussies touched.

"Oh God," Jenny gasped. "Your pussy feels so hot."

"As hot as your *girlfriend's*?"

"It's *different* with you," she said. "I've never–"

"Been on the bottom before?" I smiled.

"Not like this," she said. "I *like* being fucked by you."

As I mashed my pussy into hers, I heard the familiar sloshing sound of our wet vulvas sucking and caressing each other's lips. I grabbed her tits with my two hands and squeezed them as hard as I could, feeling my ass slide over her slick thigh as we rocked our hips together.

"Jade," Jenny growled, peering at me with wild eyes. "I'm going to cum. Oh God, I'm going to cum all over your hot pussy."

Suddenly, I felt her hips shaking underneath me as a sexy flush rolled over her face.

"Yes, Jenny," I panted. "You're so beautiful. I'm going to cum with you, baby. Oh *fuck*–"

I pulled Jenny's upturned leg hard against my chest,

feeling my pussy beginning to pulse in powerful contractions. Unable to hold it any longer, I gushed all over her slit as we wailed in delirious union. After what seemed like an eternity shaking and looking into each other's eyes while we enjoyed a long climax together, I collapsed onto the bed beside her and stroked her pretty face with the back of my hand.

"That was incredible," Jenny panted. "I don't think I've cum that hard in my whole life."

"Not even with my *Rabbit* vibrator or that funny finger-shaped sex toy?"

"Those were pretty good, I have to admit," she smiled. "But nothing like feeling your body next to mine." She looked between our legs at the huge wet spot that had formed on top of the comforter. "Plus, you've got a *special* power that none of those other devices have. That was the most stimulating shower I've had in a long time."

"There's more where that came from," I said, grinning like a Cheshire Cat. "Are you ready to try this again in a more equally yoked position?"

"Yes, but how would that work exactly?" Jenny asked. "Doesn't one of us kind of have to take the lead role when we're connected that way?"

I reached over and swung open my nightstand drawer, pulling out the long double-sided pink dildo.

"Not if something *else* is connecting us together," I smiled. "Have you had a chance to try *this* one yet?"

"I was kind of saving that one for you," Jenny said. "I figured you'd be able to show me how to use it properly."

"You got that right, girl," I smirked. "Now get up on all fours while I fuck you from behind with this thing."

"I like the sound of that," Jenny purred.

As I pressed one end of the dildo into my sopping hole and pressed my ass backwards towards hers, I tilted my head down and peered between my legs at her swinging tits.

This was one holiday I'd never soon forget, I thought to myself.

Everybody's an exhibitionist in disguise

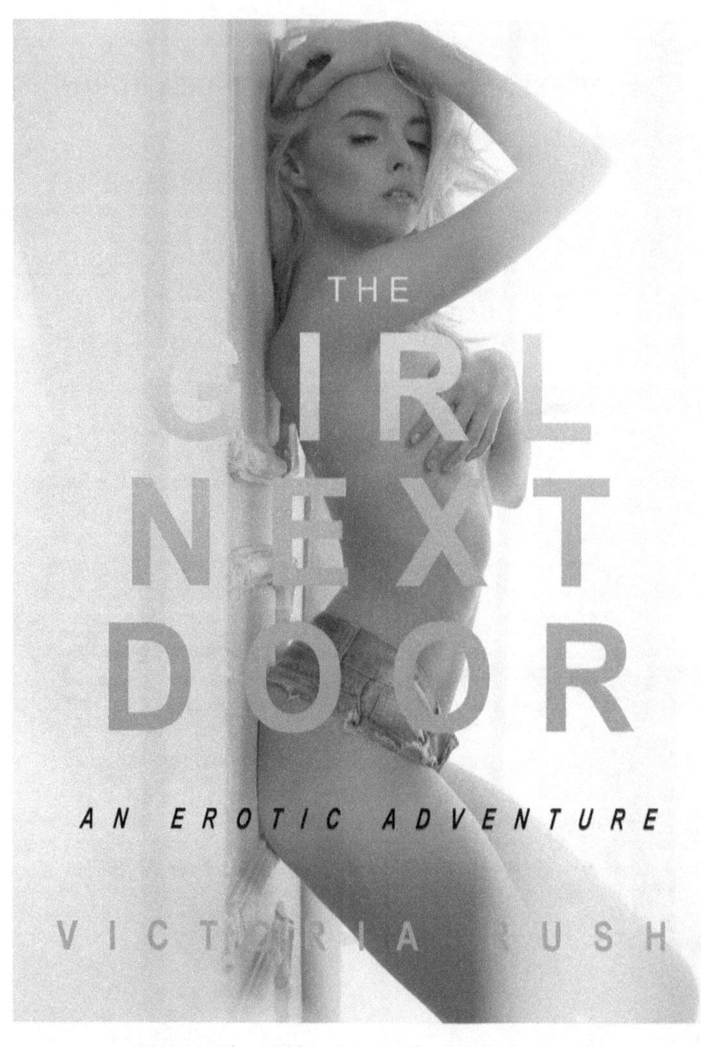

Spying on the neighbors just got a lot more interesting...

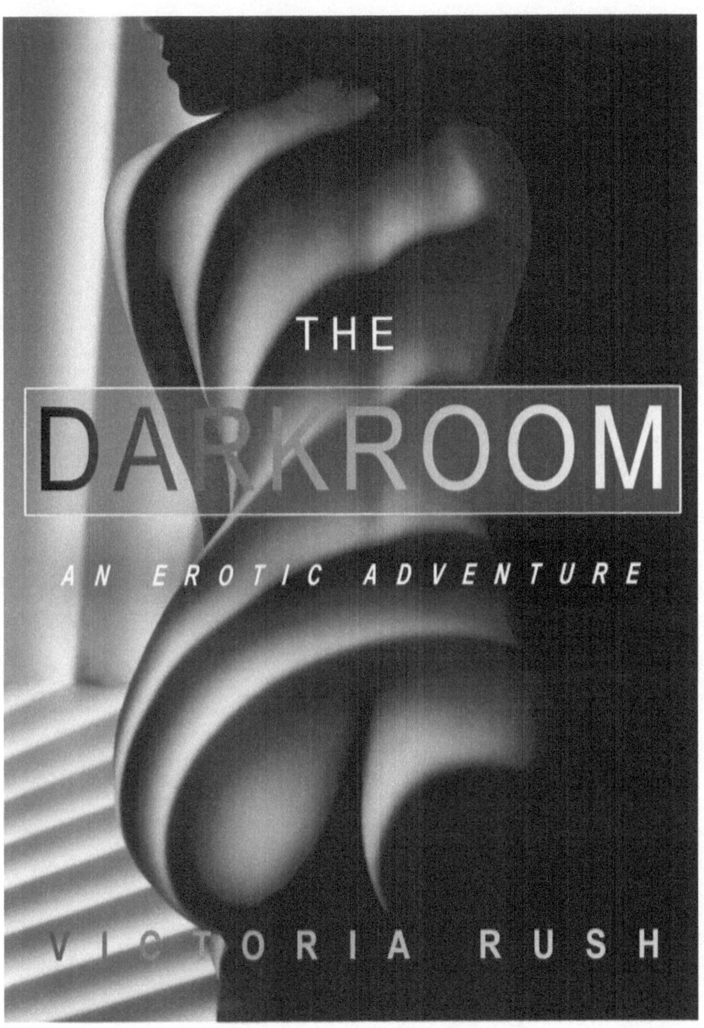

Everything's sexier in the dark...

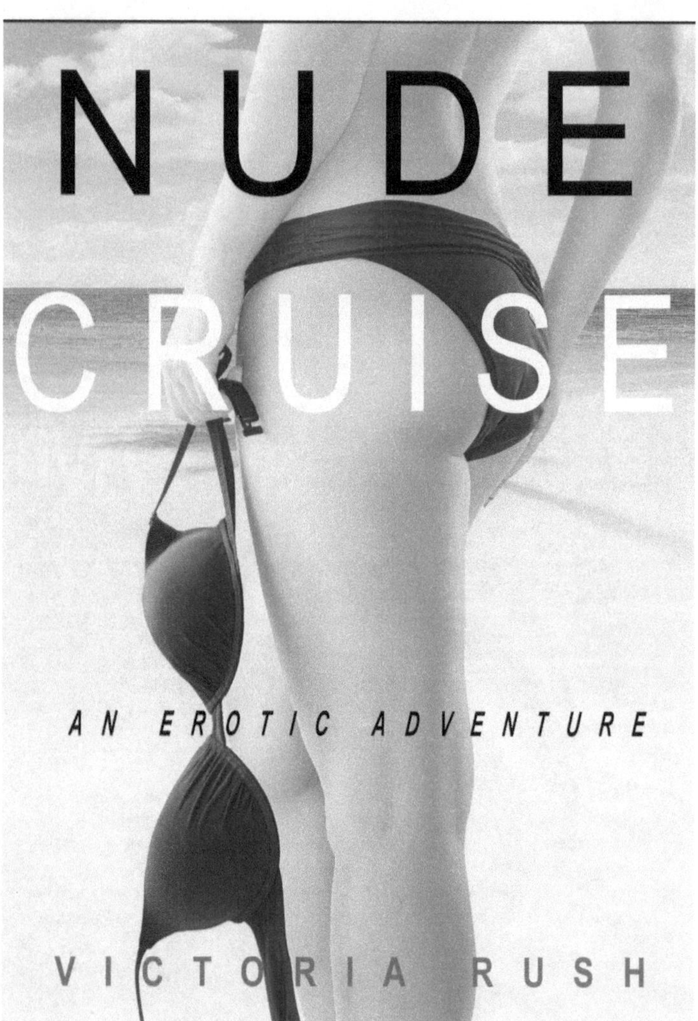

Some people get wet on a cruise for different reasons...

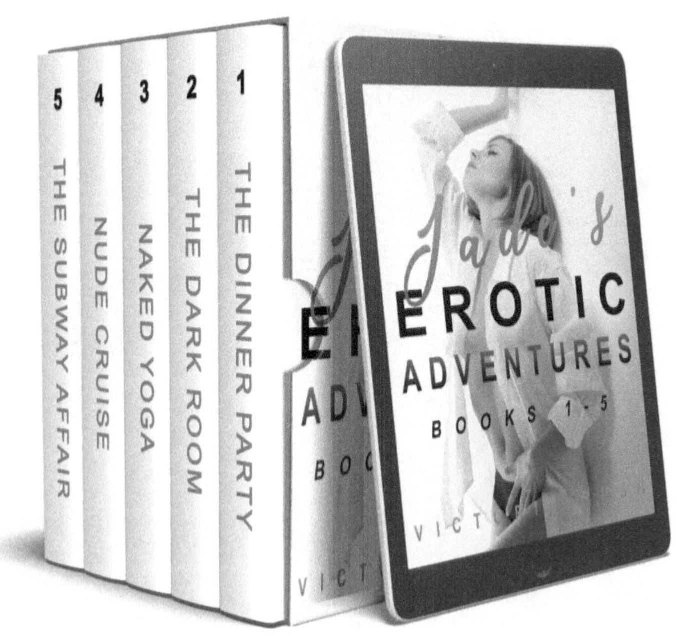

Books 1 -5 in the bestselling erotica series - 60% off

THE THERAPIST - PREVIEW
CHAPTER 1

"Every time I see you, I want to tell one of those bad gynecologist jokes," I said to my sex therapist friend Hannah at our weekly luncheon.

Hannah rolled her eyes as she took another bite of her salad. Her practice seemed to be the never-ending butt of jokes among our friends, but she'd learned to take the digs with good humor.

"Well you know I'm a far cry from a gynecologist, but I could use a little laugh today, so if you really need to get it out of your system, lay it on me."

"Ok, so this old lady goes to see her dentist," I started. "When her appointment is called, she sits in the chair, lowers her underpants, and raises her legs…"

"Uh huh," Hannah murmured, lifting a glass of soda water to her lips to signal her disinterest.

"So the dentist says," I continued, 'Excuse me, but I'm not a gynecologist.'"

I paused long enough for Hannah to begin swallowing her water. "'I know,' said the old lady. 'I want you to take my husband's teeth out.'"

Hannah lurched forward, spewing her soda water all over her salad as she raised her hand to her mouth, coughing loudly.

"Are you okay?" I said, glancing at the surrounding restaurant patrons alarmed by the sudden commotion at our table.

"Y–yeah," Hannah gagged. "The water just went down the wrong way. I wasn't expecting that punchline."

"Pretty good, right?" I smiled.

"Better than most, I'll grant you," she nodded. "But I don't know why you guys always make fun of my practice. *Someone* has to help all the sexually dysfunctional people out there."

"I know," I said, frowning sheepishly. "It's just hard to imagine what goes on in your office when people talk candidly about their sex lives."

"You'd be surprised," Hannah said, taking another swig of water to clear her throat. "In fact, I was thinking of inviting you to one of my sessions sometime."

I pinched my eyebrows and shook my head, surprised at her offer.

"As a *patient* or as an observer?"

"You don't need any help with your sex life," she said.

"You're already miles ahead of me with all your wild escapades and adventures. I'd like to present you as more of a role model for what a healthy, sexually uninhibited person looks like."

"What would you have me *do* exactly? Don't you have to protect patient-doctor privilege? I thought you guys had to keep everything at arms-length, so to speak."

"I've been experimenting with some different strategies lately," Hannah smiled. "Let's just say I've been trying out some more *active* therapeutic techniques."

"No way!" I said, widening my eyes as I rested my cocktail on the table so as not to spill it. "Isn't that against the rules? I thought you had to maintain a certain degree of professional distance or risk losing your license."

"I still do. The only difference is now I encourage them to practice some of the prescribed self-empowerment techniques in my *office* instead of at home, so I can coach and guide them more actively. Besides, everybody signs a waiver before we take it to the next level."

"Holy shit!" I said, shaking my glass incredulously. "While you *watch* them touch themselves intimately?"

"Sometimes," Hannah nodded. "But most patients prefer to be concealed behind a protective screen when they first start the process."

"So you basically guide them through a facilitated *masturbation* session?"

"In a manner of speaking, yes. I find most patients need a little more active engagement to get them over the hump becoming comfortable enjoying sex with another person. You'd be surprised how many sexually dysfunctional women there are out there."

"So most of your patients are women?"

"Yes–I find them much more interesting to work with."

"Oh my God," I panted, beginning to feel my panties moisten under my tight jeans. "I'd love to be a fly on the wall in one of these sessions. How do you manage to stay focused when things start to heat up? Don't you get aroused while these women pleasure themselves?"

Hannah shifted uncomfortably in her chair, signaling for the waiter to bring her another cocktail.

"I do. At first, I just kind of squirmed in my chair and squeezed my legs together in frustration. But I've discovered a more animated way to keep myself stimulated while I watch my patients enjoying themselves."

My eyes flew open as the fluid in my cocktail glass began to tremble.

"You stick a *vibrator* down your pants?!" I said. "Isn't that kind of noisy? How do you hide that from your patients?"

"It's not just *any* vibrator," Hannah said with a crooked grin. "Our friend Cheryl from the local Babeland store introduced me to a new kind of toy. It's designed by a woman to mimic the touch and movement of real fingers and lips. It doesn't buzz so much as *hum* as it undulates both inside and on the outside of your vulva."

"Jesus!" I squealed, furrowing my brow in frustration. "Just when I thought I had the full collection of the latest toys. What does this thing look like?"

Hannah opened up her purse and passed me a large finger-shaped device attached to a hollow cone at the base.

"I just happen to carry one with me wherever I go," she said. "See for yourself."

I peered at the strange-looking object, stroking the soft silicone surface gently.

"It sure doesn't look like anything I've seen before. How does it work if it doesn't vibrate?"

"The long finger-shaped appendage goes inside you and

bends in a series of come-hither motions against your G-spot. Give it a try by tapping the control button on the base one time."

I pressed the button and the finger began waving toward me like some kind of animatronic alien finger.

"*What the fuck*?" I said. "That's insane! It moves just like a real finger. And it hardly makes a sound."

"That the best part. You can use it anywhere. Even in a crowded restaurant. You should give it a try. Pretend that you're reclining on a couch in my office."

I glanced around the table to make sure no one else had seen the strange device that I was fondling at the table.

"It's tempting," I said, peering into the orifice at the top of the cone. "But what's with this little hole near the bottom of the device? What goes on there?"

"See for yourself," Hannah smiled. "Tap the button a second time. You might be in for a bit of a surprise."

I tapped the button again and a long, tongue-shaped object pushed up out of the hole and began undulating like a hypnotic snake against my palm.

My eyes grew wide as saucers as Hannah nodded at me with a huge smirk.

"Like I said," she grinned. "It's not a vibrator so much as a *replicator*. Doesn't it remind you of a real finger and tongue?"

"In a weird, perverted, *ET* kind of way–yeah."

Hannah lowered her gaze and nodded toward my midsection.

"You've got to feel it down there to really appreciate it. Go ahead–give it a try. No one needs to know besides us girls."

"Seriously?" I said. "Right here?!"

"Why not? There's a long skirt surrounding the table.

You can loosen your pants and insert it inside you without anyone knowing. Let me have a little bit of fun watching you pleasure yourself for a change. We haven't been together that way in quite a while."

"I have to admit," I huffed. "I *am* insanely horny right now. I'm dying to try this thing out. But what are you going to do while I amuse myself?"

"I'm going to eat my salad like we're having a normal luncheon. This is all about *you* girl, don't worry about me. Knock yourself out."

"I can't believe I'm thinking about doing this," I said, watching the tongue slither back into its hole as I turned the toy off temporarily.

"It should be pretty easy to insert it if you're already properly worked up," Hannah said, lifting her glass to her lips.

I glanced to both sides of our table to make sure nobody else was watching, then reached under the tablecloth and unzipped my jeans, pulling them down to the floor. I could feel my juices already pooling on the wooden chair between my legs as I lowered the device under the table.

"Just be sure to position it so the hole is over your clit," Hannah whispered.

"I'm all over that," I nodded, slowly inserting the bulbous tip into my opening.

It slipped inside my slit smoothly, and I gasped as I pushed it all the way up inside me.

"It's not like just *any* old finger, is it?" Hannah grinned.

"No," I panted. "It's longer and fatter than most."

"It's designed with the ideal shape and form to stimulate your G-spot. If you've got it pressed all the way inside, turn it on to see what it feels like when it's animated."

I glanced around me nervously, watching the other restaurant patrons lost in conversation with their partners.

"Are you sure I'm going to be able to control myself in full view of all these customers? What if I break out into a Meg Ryan in front of all these people?"

"That'll be up to you to keep things under control as much as you can. But if not, what's the worst that can happen? Just like in the movie, everybody will want to know what you ordered that made you so happy."

"Very funny," I said, fumbling to find the control button on the base of the unit resting over my mound.

I pressed the button and began squirming in my chair as the long pointed finger began caressing me like no lover I ever had.

"Uhnn," I groaned, feeling the unusual stimulation inside my pussy.

"Not too bad, is it?" Hannah smiled. "Imagine all that going on while you're watching one of my patients pleasuring themselves."

"Is that really *possible*?" I said, getting even more turned on at the thought of watching one of her clients playing with herself in Hannah's private office.

"I've been thinking about it for a while," Hannah nodded. "It's the logical next step in the process of learning to become fully functional in a paired relationship. I've already had a few of my patients suggest they'd like me to guide them through their first encounter with another partner."

"You know how I like to *watch*," I groaned, as my eyes began to glaze over from the delicate sensation of the long finger rubbing up against my G-spot.

Hannah crossed her legs under the table and began to

bob up and down as she flexed her buttocks and thighs together watching me get off.

"I do," she said, lifting her cocktail glass off the table and sliding her tongue around the rim suggestively. "Try the tongue action now."

"You're such a tease," I hissed, reaching under the table-cloth and tapping the control button one more time.

When I felt the flexible appendage push out of the hole and begin rolling over my hard clit, I bent over my place setting, grasping the handles of my chair tightly.

"That's it, babe," Hannah purred. "Feel the rhythm. Close your eyes and imagine it's your fantasy partner licking your pussy. Surrender to the feeling..."

"Is this how you do it with your clients?" I panted. "Talking to them all sexy while they play with themselves?"

"Sometimes," Hannah smiled. "Or sometimes I just let them do most of the vocalization while they tell me what they're doing behind the screen."

I spread my knees further apart imagining myself in one of her sessions.

"Do they ever get to the point where they're comfortable letting you watch them?"

"That's the ultimate goal. I've had a number of clients reach that level already. But I'd like to try taking it one step further. That's where you come in—"

"Tell me, Han," I moaned, beginning to lose myself in the fantasy. "Tell me what you want me to do with your sexy patients."

"We'll start out slowly at first," she instructed. "We'll just have you listen to them moan and purr as they begin the process of self-discovery behind the safety of their protective screen. But you'll have to be quiet at first to not distract their self-focus."

"At *this* point," I said, beginning to feel the pleasure spreading over my entire body. "That might be enough. With this amazing device doing its thing, I could probably get off listening to the sound of running water."

"That's the intent," Hannah laughed. "At least for my clients. But in order for them to become truly uninhibited and be able to function competently, the next step would be for the two of you to emerge from your hiding places and become comfortable watching each other in a face-to-face setting."

"*Fuck, yes,*" I panted. "If I can help another soul learn to enjoy the full pleasures of lesbian sex, count me in!"

"I know *you* won't have any trouble participating in this next phase of the process," Hannah smiled. "Just try to keep some of your more extreme methods in check for a while so you don't scare away my customers."

"I promise to keep my big dildos at home if you insist," I smirked.

"Once we get them feeling comfortable touching themselves and achieving climax in this voyeur scenario, the last step will be for the two of you to join together on the same couch and explore each other with more direct contact."

"Can I break out some of my favorite moves then?"

"If you find your partner is responding appropriately. Just be careful to always be gentle and focused on her needs. If you get to the point where she feels comfortable getting more inventive, by all means–"

"Oh, I've got the *means* alright," I moaned, imaging myself straddling one of her patients with her legs splayed wide apart as we ground our pussies together and I watched her come all over me. "How soon can we set this up?"

"I've got a certain patient in mind. She's young and never been with another woman before. She's had some unfulfilling experiences with men and confided that she's always fantasized about being with a woman. We'll just have to ease her into it carefully. Are you up for the opportunity, assuming she's game?"

"You know I am," I grunted, pressing harder down against the artificial tongue. "But first, tell me more about this girl..."

"She's nineteen, a sophomore in college, with a cheerleader's body–"

"She's athletic then?"

"Oh yes," Hannah smiled. "Tight ass, firm tits, and legs that could wrap all the way around you while you tribbed her virgin pussy–"

"Oh God, Han," I moaned. "I can't take it any longer. Sign me up–I want to taste her sweet pussy in my mouth..."

"Yes, Jade," Hannah purred. "Let it go, hun. Surrender to the feeling–"

As I imagined the co-ed writhing in ecstasy sitting on my face, the pleasure generated by the lifelike sex toy suddenly peaked, and I bit my lip as I began convulsing in my chair. I'd never fought so hard to remain quiet during a powerful orgasm in my entire life. There was something about the experience of cumming surrounded by scores of oblivious restaurant patrons that made the experience all the more erotic. While I twisted and squirmed in my chair, Hannah smiled as she raised her glass in toast to me.

"Congratulations, Jade," she said. "You've just passed the first test with flying colors."

READ MORE...

ABOUT THE AUTHOR

If you would like to receive notification of new book(s) in Jade's Erotic Adventures, follow me at http://bookbub.com/authors/victoria-rush.

If you have a moment, please post a brief review on my Amazon book page at viewbook.at/thehousesitter . Even just a couple of sentences will help other readers find and enjoy this book as much as you hopefully did.

Follow, share, like, and comment at:

www.facebook.com/authorvictoriarush
www.pinterest.com/authorvictoriarush
www.twitter.com/authorvictoriarush
authorvictoriarush@outlook.com

Hope to see you again soon!

www.ingramcontent.com/pod-product-compliance
Lightning Source LLC
Chambersburg PA
CBHW030822200726

48288CB00004B/1351